OF

DOCTOR BOOX

The extraordinary
adventures
of Doctor Boox,
the greatest
animal doctor
in the world!
Featuring a
lost gorilla,
a boxing kangaroo,
sinking ducks
and a giraffe
with a sore neck . . .

Also by Andrew Davies
in Magnet Books

Educating Marmalade
Danger – Marmalade at Work!
Marmalade Atkins in Space
Marmalade Atkins' Dreadful Deeds
Marmalade Hits the Big Time

The Fantastic Feats

of Doctor Boox

Andrew Davies

Illustrated by Tony Escott

A Magnet Book

First published in this edition 1985
by Methuen Children's Books Ltd
This Magnet paperback published 1987
by Methuen Children's Books Ltd
11 New Fetter Lane, London EC4P 4EE
Text copyright © 1972 Andrew Davies
Illustrations copyright © 1972 Tony Escott
First published in Great Britain 1972
by William Collins Sons & Co Ltd
All rights reserved
Printed in Great Britain
by Richard Clay Ltd, Bungay, Suffolk

ISBN 0 416 03132 3

To William and Anna

CONTENTS

DOCTOR BOOX
AND
THE SORE
GIRAFFE

My friend Doctor Boox, the animal doctor, lives in a big house with rather a lot of animals: dogs, cats, lizards, goats, and so on. Doctor Boox is not the cleverest man in the world, but he does his best. Well: this is the story about Boox and the sore giraffe.

One morning, rather late, Doctor Boox was lying in bed with a few dogs and hamsters, when the telephone rang.

"Boox here," said Boox. "What do you want?"

"Schmitt itty Shoo Shah," said the telephone.

"Can't hear a word you're saying," said Boox. This was because he had his stethoscope stuck in his ears. He always kept it there to be on the safe side. He took it off and gave it to a dog to hold.

"This is the Zoo," said the telephone. "We've got a sore giraffe here."

"Where is it sore?" said Boox.

"In the neck," said the man on the telephone.

"Oh dear," said Boox. "I was afraid of that."

"Well, can you help?"

"Oh, I'll have a go," said Boox. He put the phone down.

"Right lads," said Boox to the dogs. "We're off to the Zoo."

"Row! Row! Row!" shouted the dogs.

They went downstairs to Doctor Boox's red sports car and they all got in. Three of the dogs sat on Boox's knee. "Move over lads," said Boox. "Let the dog see the rabbit." And then they were off. Boox drove very fast because it was an emergency.

On the way, he had an idea. He was no fool, and as he had not had dealings with any giraffes before, he thought he would practise on a lamppost. So he parked his car by one of the biggest lampposts in town.

"Let's see," said Boox. And he took a quick run at the lamppost and went up it in three jumps and a scramble.

"Easy!" said Boox. "Pretty good, eh lads?" But when he looked down at the dogs in the car they seemed a long way down and Doctor Boox began to get frightened. He clung very tight to the lamppost.

"Row! Row! Row!" shouted the dogs. They wanted him to get down, but Boox

didn't know how to get down.

Just then, a policeman came along. "What are you doing up there?" he said.

"Training," said Boox. "I've got to get up a giraffe this morning."

"A likely tale," said the policeman. "Get down at once!"

"I can't," said Boox. "I'm frightened."
So the policeman went away and got the
fire brigade.

Soon the red fire engine came along. "I
thought you were never coming," said
Boox.

The firemen hoisted the big ladder, and
Boox stepped very carefully on to it.
"Thanks very much," he said. Then he
had another idea.

"I'll tell you what," he said. "What
about taking me to the Zoo?"

"All right," said the fireman, who had nothing better to do that morning.

So all the dogs got in the fire engine, and the firemen drove to the Zoo, with Boox still on the ladder.

"This is the life," said Boox to himself, as they whizzed through the town with the bells ringing.

When they got to the Zoo they drove straight up to the giraffe, who was very sore indeed now, and rather cross. But Boox got out his bottle of liniment (on the label it said DOCTOR BOOX'S DOUBLE STRENGTH NECK RUB) and rubbed the

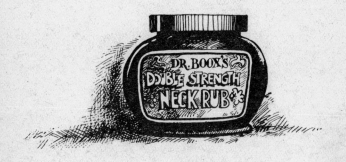

giraffe's neck with it. After a bit the giraffe said:

"Ahhhhh."

"He's better now," said Boox.

"Thank you very much," said the Zoo man.

"Good old Boox," said the firemen.

"Row! row! row!" said the dogs.

"Don't mention it," said Boox. "Anybody like to come back to my house for a snack?"

They all got into the fire engine and went back to Doctor Boox's house where they all had lemonade and three biscuits each out of Doctor Boox's big biscuit barrel.

Except Boox.

Boox had five biscuits because he thought he owed it to himself after his busy morning.

DOCTOR BOOX

AND

THE SINKING

DUCKS

One day last week (Tuesday actually) Doctor Boox woke up earlier than usual (about ten o'clock actually). He pushed off some dogs who were lying on top of him and sat up in bed. The sun was shining.

"No work today lads!" said Boox to the dogs. "We'll have a day off."

The dogs just lay about on the bed and said nothing.

"We'll go to the park," said Boox. "How about that?"

"Row row row!" said the dogs, and they all got up and ran downstairs and got into Boox's red sports car.

When they got to the park, they wondered what to do. First they all went down the slide, then they all went on the climbing frame, then the dogs took turns pushing Doctor Boox on the swing. They soon got tired, because Doctor Boox was rather fat and heavy, and he liked to go very high on the swing. When the last dog was tired out, Boox got off the swing and said: "I know lads. Let's get a boat and go for a row on the lake." They had to get the biggest boat of all, because there were so many of them.

Boox took the oars, and they set off. They did not go very fast because Boox was not very good at rowing. Soon he was very hot. This is worse than work, he said to

himself. The dogs were having a good time, though, lying on their backs with their tongues out, trailing their tails in the water. "All right for you," said Boox.

Then he had an idea.

"Get up, lads!" he said. "Call yourselves dogs, don't you? Right, paddle!"

So the dogs leaned over the side and paddled, and soon the boat was going quite fast. "This is more like it," said Boox to himself. Then he heard someone shouting. It was the park-keeper.

"Doctor Boox! Doctor Boox!"

"I'm not Boox!" said Boox.

"Yes you are!"

"Well, it's my day off," said Boox.

"But the ducks are sinking!" shouted the park-keeper. Boox had a look. The ducks

were sinking. Some of them had their wings under water and some of them had their tails under water, and some of them had sunk so far that you could only see their beaks!

"Astonishing!" said Boox. "Quick, lads, out of the boat!"

The dogs all jumped out of the boat and carried the ducks over to the island, where they lay on the ground puffing and blowing. Boox got out his stethoscope and examined them. "These ducks are full of something very heavy," he said. "That's why they are sinking."

"Clever chap," said the park-keeper.

"Row row row!" said the dogs.

"But what are they full of, eh?" said Boox. "Search the island, lads!"

The dogs ran all over the island, and quite soon they found a boy with a big sack.

"What's in the sack?" said Boox.

"Granny's bread pudding," said the boy. "I've only been feeding the ducks."

"Well," said Boox, "you'll have to pack it in. They're all sinking."

"All right," said the boy. "But. . . ."

"But what?" said Boox.

"What can I do with Granny's bread pudding? She makes enough for a sackful every day and I don't know what to do with it."

"I think I can help you there," said Boox. "I'm fond of a bit of bread pudding myself."

"So am I," said the park-keeper.

"Row row row!" said the dogs.

So now every afternoon the boy, whose name is Antony, brings a sack of Granny's bread pudding to Boox's house, and Boox and the park-keeper and the dogs eat it all up. They all eat a lot, but Boox eats the most. He says he doesn't worry about sinking because he never goes swimming.

DOCTOR BOOX
AND
THE ESCAPED
GORILLA

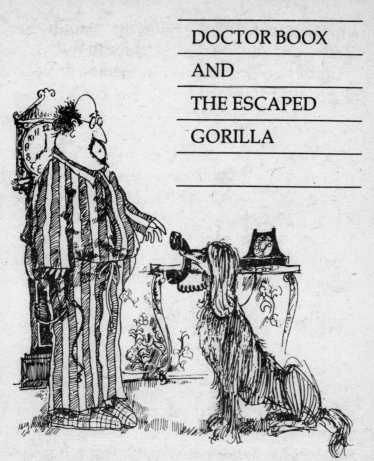

One morning Doctor Boox was, as usual, lying about in bed with some of his dogs when the telephone rang. Boox just gave a great snore and rolled over, but a clever dog called Towzer picked up the telephone in his teeth, and all the other dogs shouted "Row row row!" to wake Doctor Boox up.

"Boox here," said Boox, remembering to take the stethoscope out of his ear.

"This is the London Zoo," said the telephone.

"I might have known it," said Boox. "What do you want this time?"

"Do you know anything about gorillas?" said the Zoo man.

"I've known one or two," said Boox in a doubtful way. "Like big monkeys, aren't they?" (Actually Boox knew a whole lot about gorillas, but he didn't like to spread it around.)

. "That's right," said the Zoo man. "Well, one of our gorillas has escaped from the Zoo, and we want you to help us find him."

"I was having a sleep," said Boox, who was in a bad mood.

"*Please*, Doctor Boox," said the Zoo man. "We're very worried at the Zoo."

"Oh, all right, I'll have a look round," said Boox, and he put the phone down.

"Right, lads, into the car," he said. "And look out for anything hairy!"

"Row row row!" said the dogs, and away they roared in Boox's noisy red sports car. Boox thought he would go to

Regents Park first, because it was full of the kind of trees that gorillas like, and anyway Boox liked to watch the ducks there.

But on the way to the park he began to feel extremely hungry, and he remembered that he had not had his breakfast yet. "No wonder I'm in a bad mood," he thought to himself. "I'm all empty." Just then he saw a cafe he sometimes went to and he stopped the car with a jerk.

"Wait here, lads," he said to the dogs. "I won't be a minute."

"Large lemonade and four custard cream biscuits," he said to the lady in the cafe.

"Here's your lemonade," said the lady. "But we're out of custard creams."

"What?" shouted Boox. "But I haven't had breakfast! I'm empty, madam!"

"I'm very sorry," said the lady. "But the gentleman had them all."

"What gentleman?" said Boox.

"The one in the hairy overcoat!"

Boox looked round. There was a lady in a straw hat eating jelly; and there was a man in a pork pie hat eating pork pies; and

there was a boy in a striped cap eating
ice-cream. But right in the corner, there was
a huge person in a very hairy overcoat

indeed, with a huge pile of custard cream
biscuits. Doctor Boox had a good look at
him. He had hairy trousers as well. And
hairy gloves. And hairy shoes. And a hairy
face. Boox was no fool, as we know. He
thought to himself: "something funny

here, Boox." And he sat down with the hairy person.

"Excuse me," he said to the hairy person, "but I think you're a gorilla on the quiet."

"Ugrumph," said the gorilla in a friendly way. Boox was right again.

"Come out to the car," said Boox. "I've got something to interest you in the boot." The gorilla finished his biscuits and they shambled out of the cafe.

When they got to the car Boox made all the dogs squash into the back seat on top of each other, with their tails sticking over the back, and sat the gorilla in front with him. Then he opened the boot and got out his tin of special emergency travelling biscuits, and gave them to the gorilla.

"Row row row!" said the dogs, and they set off for the Zoo.

When they got there, all the Zoo men gave a great cheer.

"Boox has done it again!" they said.

"Row row row!" said the dogs.

"Ugrumph," said the gorilla.

"Don't mention it," said Boox.

But when they opened the cage with its big bars, the gorilla wouldn't go in. They pushed and shoved, and they threw biscuits in the cage, but still the gorilla would not move.

"He wants to stay with you," said the Zoo man to Doctor Boox.

"You must be joking," said Boox, with an uneasy laugh.

"You can have him," said the Zoo man.

"But I don't *need* a gorilla," said Boox.

The gorilla put his arms round Boox and started to cry. Boox couldn't stand it.

"Oh, all right," said Boox. And the gorilla got back into the car.

THE
GORILLA

"No more work today," said Boox when they got home, and they spent the afternoon playing football in the garden. The gorilla was in goal, and when the ball went in a tree, he just shambled up and threw it down. They all had a great time.

36

Soon it was the dogs' bedtime, but Boox and the gorilla sat up very late in two armchairs drinking lemonade, and Doctor

Boox opened a new barrel of biscuits. The gorilla didn't say much, but Boox didn't mind: he told the gorilla some stories about his early days in Africa. After a while the

gorilla went to sleep. Boox tucked him up with four rugs, and went off to bed, feeling very happy. "I didn't know it," he said to himself, "but a gorilla was just what I could do with."

DOCTOR BOOX

AND

THE SLOW

GREYHOUND

One day Doctor Boox was driving his red sports car along Battersea Park Road. He had four or five of his dogs with him, all lolling about the car snoring. They had been to the common for a game with some dogs they knew, and they were all very tired. Boox was tired too and looking forward to some biscuits, but he sat up straight when he saw something strange by the side of the road.

There was a fat man with a bowler hat and a thin man in a flat cap and they were both very red in the face and bad-tempered looking. They were trying to pull something out of the back of a van.

"Come out! Come out!" they were shouting.

"Wake up, lads," said Boox. "Something funny here." And he stopped the car.

"What have you got there?" he said.

"A no good greyhound," said the fat man. "We're taking him to the Dogs' Home but he won't come out."

"Right lads," said Boox. "Into the van."

Four dogs jumped into the van, and after a lot of grunting and sniffling five dogs fell out in a heap. Boox's dogs got back in the car and there stood a beautiful white greyhound. The greyhound looked at Boox and gave a great yawn.

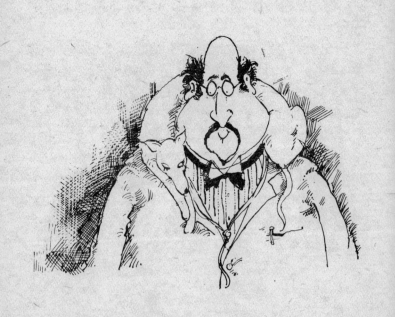

"He looks all right to me," said Boox. "What's the matter with him?"

"He's a slow greyhound," said the fat man. "He comes last in all the races."

"And he's eating us out of house and home," said the thin man, looking hungrily at Boox's tin of travelling biscuits.

"So we're getting rid of him," said the fat man.

Boox thought for a minute.

"I'll tell you what," he said. "I'll take him off your hands."

"Well, I don't know about that," said the fat man.

"Funny how you get peckish around this time of day," said the thin man, looking at the biscuits. Boox gave him the biscuits.

"It's a deal," said the man. They got back in the van and Boox drove home with the dogs. The greyhound was draped gracefully round his shoulders and Boox felt as warm and cosy as if he had a fur coat on.

The next evening Boox decided to see how slow the beautiful greyhound was. He put him in for a race. The race was at the White City Stadium and all the fast dogs were there. Boox and the gorilla sat in the best seats to watch the race, eating biscuits and drinking lemonade.

All the dogs got into little cages ready for the race. Boox's greyhound was the last to go in. He was in Trap 5 and he had a little coat with 5 on it. Then a man pressed a button and the electric toy rabbit started whizzing round the track. When it came past the greyhounds, the gates opened and they all whizzed after it as fast as they could go.

All except Boox's dog. He came lolloping out very slowly and sleepily last of all. He took one look at the rabbit, yawned, turned round three times, and lay down. All the people watching laughed.

"The slow greyhound's back!" they shouted.

That night in bed Boox couldn't go to sleep. He was worrying about the slow greyhound. What could be making him so lackadaisical?

Then he heard noises from downstairs. There were bangs and crashes and shouts and car noises ... and barks. Loud greyhoundish sort of barks.

"Hum hum," said Boox to himself. "I think we're on to something." And he went downstairs.

There on the sofa sat the slow greyhound, bouncing up and down and barking his head off with excitement. He was watching the Late Night Movie on television.

"So that's it," said Boox. "No wonder you're such a slow greyhound if you sneak downstairs and watch television till one o'clock in the morning! Go to bed at once."

The next morning the slow greyhound got up very late and yawned all day, but Boox knew why. That evening he waited till ten to nine when his favourite programme was over (it had a police dog in it and the greyhound thought it was great) then he pulled the plug out of the set and said, "No more telly tonight." The greyhound went off to bed looking rather sad.

The next evening Boox put him in another race. When the gates opened the greyhound came out very fast indeed but just near the end of the race he started yawning and he finished third.

"I think we're on the right lines now," said Boox to the gorilla.

Next day he called all the dogs round him.

"No telly after six o'clock from now on lads!" he said, and all that week he pulled the plug out as soon as the children's pro grammes were over. Boox was missing all his favourite programmes but it gave him a chance to catch up on his reading and woodwork. And the greyhound was getting friskier and friskier.

Saturday was the day of the Greyhound Gold Cup race. Boox put the greyhound in for it and took all the other dogs and the gorilla to watch. They sat in the best seats eating biscuits and drinking lemonade. When the gates opened Boox's greyhound came out like a rocket! He zoomed past all the other dogs!

"Look at the slow greyhound!" shouted all the people.

"He's the fastest greyhound now," said Boox.

He won the race easily and Boox was presented with the Gold Cup. He filled it up with milk for the greyhound to drink. Everybody was shouting and cheering.

"Boox, you're a marvel!"

"Oh, it was nothing," said Boox modestly.

Then up came the fat man in the bowler hat and the thin man in the flat cap. They took their hat and cap off.

"Er, Dr Boox," said the fat man. "Could we have our dog back?"

"I don't know about that," said Boox. But he could see the greyhound wagging his tail.

"We do miss him," said the thin man.

"Funny how quick the biscuits run out," said Boox meaningly.

The thin man got out a barrel of biscuits he had ready.

"Well, all right," said Boox. "But keep him away from the telly."

The greyhound jumped into the van.

"Row row," he said.

"Row row," said Boox's dogs.

"Cheerio," said Boox.

"Grumph," said the gorilla.

Well, the fat man and the thin man must have looked after him and kept him away from the telly, because he still wins all his races. If you ever go to a greyhound race look out for him. He goes like a rocket!

DOCTOR BOOX

AND

THE BOXING

KANGAROO

One morning Dr Boox came down to breakfast late as usual, and found to his dismay that he had *completely run out of biscuits.*

"This is disastrous!" he shouted. "Quick, lads, into the car!" All the dogs rushed to the car, the gorilla opened the garage doors, and they all set off for the supermarket moaning and groaning because they were so hungry.

Boox parked the car outside the supermarket and got out with the dogs and the gorilla. "Full speed to the biscuit counter, lads!" he said. But just as they got to the door, he stopped and frowned. Something peculiar was going on. There were a lot of bangs and thumps and a lot of shouts and screams coming from inside.

Just then a man came flying out of the door and landed with a thump at Boox's feet.

"What's going on?" said Boox.

"Help! Help!" shouted the man, and ran off down the street.

"Hum," said Boox to himself. "We'd better play it crafty."

"Go and see what's going on, Towzer," he said to his cleverest dog.

Towzer went into the supermarket, sniffing and snuffling.

There was a short pause.

Then out of the door flew Towzer. The gorilla just managed to catch him.

"What happened?" said Boox.

"Row row ooh ooh ooh," said Towzer in a frightened voice.

"Hum," said Boox. "You have a lie down in the car, Towzer. This smacks of kangaroo to me." He turned to the gorilla.

"Let's go," he said, in a brave voice.

Hand in hand, Boox and the gorilla went into the supermarket. There was nobody in sight, but there was some thumping from the direction of the meat counter. They turned the corner, and there was an enormous kangaroo in boxing gloves, bouncing up and down and throwing sausages about.

"I was right!" said Boox. "This is a boxing kangaroo from a circus! Do you think you could get him in a grip?"

The gorilla beat his chest a bit, then set

off bravely, shuffling round the kangaroo like an all-in wrestler. Just as he was about to spring, the kangaroo bounced up and gave him a thump on his hairy chest.

"Oogh!" said the gorilla, sitting down and looking anxiously at Boox. The kangaroo bounced up and down and got ready for another thump.

Then Boox had a brilliant idea. He rushed to the door and set the burglar alarm going.

As soon as the kangaroo heard the bell, he pricked up his ears, stopped bouncing and thumping, sat down at one of the cash desks, fanned his snout with a plastic bag.

The gorilla was amazed.

"Boxing kangaroo, see," said Boox modestly. "When he hears the bell he thinks the fight's over. He'll be all right now."

Then the manager and all the assistants came out of the cupboards they'd been hiding in.

"Boox," they said. "You've done it again!"

"Row row row," said the dogs.

"Well," said Boox. "I'd better take him back to the circus." He took the kangaroo's paw, and led him out to the car. The manager came rushing out with two barrels of biscuits.

"Please accept these with my compliments," he said.

Boox was just loading them into the boot when he heard *another* alarm bell. It was from the bank over the road. Three men came running out with guns and big bags of stolen money. Bank robbers!

The kangaroo bounced up and down and started thumping the sides of the car.

"Quick!" said Boox. "Point him in the right direction!"

The gorilla pointed him at the bank robbers, and with three quick thumps the robbers had been knocked down and the moneybags were lying in the road.

"Ring your bell!" said Boox to a boy on a bicycle.

The boy rang his bell and the kangaroo sat down for a rest.

Then two vans drove up. One van was the police van to take the robbers away and the other van was the circus van out looking for the kangaroo.

The kangaroo looked very pleased to see his trainer again.

Boox and the gorilla watched him bounce into the van.

"He was a good kangaroo as kangaroos go," said Boox thoughtfully. "But to tell the truth I'm not altogether sorry to see the back of him."

DOCTOR BOOX,
GRUNTY ANNA,
AND
THE LORRY
OF PIGS

One day Boox was out for a drive in his red sports car. The gorilla was sitting in the front seat as usual, toying with a banana. But there were fewer dogs than usual. In fact there were only two: Towzer the clever one, and a rather pale dog called Humphrey who needed all the fresh air he could get. The rest of the space was taken up by a boy called William and his sister Anna.

William was four and a half and he talked all the time. Anna was only one and she didn't talk at all. She just grunted. OINK. Like that.

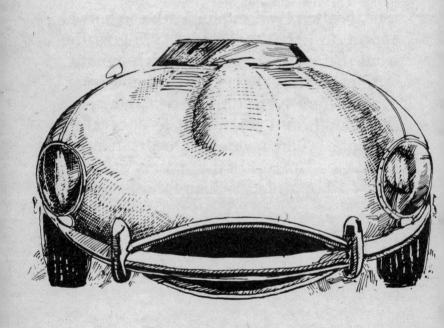

As Boox drove along William said the names of all the cars they passed. He knew nearly all of them.

"That's a Metro," he said. "That's a Fiesta. That's a 2CV. That's a Volvo." When he didn't know the names he made them up.

"That's an Extrensor," he said. "That's a Thunderboom. That's a Crably."

Just then a long low sports car came up behind and went past Boox's red car in a rush. William jumped up and down.

"That's an E-type Jaguar!" he shouted. "They're my best cars!"

"Hum," said Boox in a grumpy voice, because he thought his car was the best in the world. "What's your favourite car, Anna?"

"OINK!" said Anna.

William thought that was very funny.

"What's your favourite pudding, grunty Anna?" he asked.

"OINK!" said Anna.

William laughed so much he nearly fell out of the car.

Then Boox turned into a narrow street. He had to drive very slowly because in front of him, taking up nearly all the road, was a very big, very old, very slow lorry. It rattled and swayed and big clouds of black smoke came from underneath. The gorilla started to cough and Humphrey looked as if he was going to be sick.

"What d'you think could be in that lorry?" said Boox.

"Must be a heavy load."

"I think it's potatoes," said William.
"What do you think, grunty Anna?"

"OINK!" said Anna.

Just as she said that, there was a loud
bang. The big door at the back of the lorry
burst open and out jumped about twenty
pigs!

Boox stopped his car with a screech of
brakes as the pigs ran about in all direc-
tions. Two men jumped out of the lorry

and started to shout at the pigs and wave their arms about but the pigs took no notice at all of that.

They ran down the street, into people's gardens, and into all the shops.

"Give us a hand Doctor Boox," said the pig men.

"Do my best," said Boox. "Out of the car lads."

The gorilla and the two dogs jumped out
and started to round up the pigs. Most of
the pigs jumped straight back into the lorry

when they saw the gorilla beating his chest, and Towzer and Humphrey rounded up the rest of them. The pig men closed the big doors and tied them up with string. The lorry was just about to start when a woman came running down the street shouting.

"Quick! Quick!" she shouted. "There's a terrible great pig in my bathroom!"

The pig men looked at each other. "Grouser," they said. "We forgot Grouser."

"Who's Grouser?" asked Boox.

"The big fierce boar," said the pig men. "Once he gets in a bathroom there's no getting him out."

"Well, I won't have it!" said the woman. So Boox and the woman and the two pig men and the gorilla and dogs and William and Anna went back up the road and into the house and up the stairs. Boox pushed the bathroom door open very gently and there on the bathmat was the biggest pig he had ever seen. He looked fierce too. Towzer and Humphrey were so frightened that they ran straight into the garden.

"That's Grouser," said the pig men.

Everybody tried to think what to do.

"I could send the gorilla in," said Boox. But the gorilla shook his head and started to go downstairs.

"Shall we try him with some biscuits?" said William.

"I'm going to ring up the fire brigade," said the lady.

But before anyone could do anything, Anna let go of William's hand and walked across the landing, into the bathroom, and right up to the big fierce pig.

And Anna said: "OINK!" The pig looked at Anna.

Then he said: "OINK!"

"OINK OINK," said Anna.

"OINK OINK," said Grouser in a friendly voice.

Then Anna took him carefully by the ear and led him down the stairs and into the garden and down the street and back to the lorry. Everyone else followed very quietly. When they got to the lorry the pig man opened the door. Anna gave Grouser a pat, and he jumped straight into the lorry.

"I'm flabbergasted," said Boox.
"What a clever girl," said William.
"Row row row," said the dogs.
But Anna just said: "OINK!"

DOCTOR BOOX
AND
THE LAMBTON
WORM

One morning Doctor Boox looked out of the window. It was foggy.

"Back to bed, lads," he said. It was always his way on foggy days. He was just getting his pyjamas back on when the phone rang. He took no notice but it went on ringing, so he picked it up.

"This is long distance from Middlesbrough," said the telephone. "You must come up here right away."

"I was just going to bed," said Boox. "It's the middle of the night down here, you know. What's the matter anyway?"

"We're having a lot of trouble with a Worm," said the telephone.

Boox had a think. A worm would be no trouble to a man who could deal with boxing kangaroos and sore giraffes, he thought.

"Well, all right, if it's just a worm, I'll come up right away with a worm powder," he said.

"It's a big one," said the telephone.

"Don't you worry," said Boox. "Right lads! Who wants a trip to the North?"

Boox drove straight to Kings Cross with the gorilla and a few dogs and soon they were all lolling about in the restaurant car as the express train rattled along towards Middlesbrough. As they got nearer Middlesbrough Boox noticed great dark clouds in the sky and a red glow in the distance.

"Funny weather we're having," he said to the gorilla.

Then the train drew up at the station. The Mayor and Council and the Chief Constable were waiting for Boox.

"Oh Doctor Boox, Doctor Boox," they said. "We're so glad to see you!"

"Never mind that," said Boox. "Where's this worm of yours?"

"On top of the hill, I'll take you," said the Chief Constable. "He's come down from Lambton to terrorize us!"

So Boox and the gorilla and dogs got into the Chief Constable's car. The Chief Constable drove to the bottom of the hill where all the smoke was coming from. Then he stopped, and pointed with a trembling finger.

"Up there," he said. Boox looked.

On the top of the hill, in the middle of all the smoke, he could just see an enormous creature about the size of a row of bungalows, covered with black shiny scales. It had paws like mechanical diggers, red eyes the size of colour television sets, and fire was coming out of its mouth.

"I don't call that a worm!" said Boox. "I call that a dragon!"

"Well," said the Chief Constable, "we call them worms hereabouts."

Fooled again, thought Boox.

"Right then," he said to the gorilla. "Let's see what's what." The gorilla looked nervous.

"The thing with these worms," said Boox, making it up as he went along, "is to let 'em know who's master. Let's take a picnic up in the haversack."

So the gorilla took some bread and
cheese in a haversack and they strolled up
the hill. The Worm watched them coming.
When they were nearly at the top of the hill
it stretched its long neck and said:

"WWWUURRRRRRRAAAAAAAAAGH!!"
and shot a long flame towards them.

Quick as a flash, Boox whipped out a cigar and put it in his mouth. The end of the flame just touched it, and Boox puffed hard.

"Thanks a lot," he said. "Rotten weather we're having."

The Worm blinked its huge red eyes twice.

"Get out the bread," whispered Boox. The gorilla took two slices of bread out of his haversack, and held them up.

"Gently now," said Boox to the Worm, and put a finger to his lips. The Worm blinked again and looked at the bread.

Then it made a soft whispering sort of roar:

"Wurrrrrrhhhhhhhh ..." and blew a very gentle flame out towards the bread, which turned a beautiful golden brown. Toast!

Boox held up his hands. "Just right," he said. The dragon blinked his eyes, lay down, and sighed quietly. The leaves on a nearby tree turned brown.

"The trouble with this Worm," said Boox, "is that nobody wants him." He had a think. "But who *does* need the Lambton Worm?"

Just then he heard the tramp tramp tramp of a lot of boots at the bottom of the hill. It was the men from the steelworks.

"What's the matter?" shouted Boox.

"Closed down today," said the men. "No fuel for the furnaces!"

"Aha," said Boox. "I think I can help you there."

"Come with me," he said to the Worm. "And try to keep your mouth shut on the way."

When they got to the steelworks Boox led the Worm down to the cellars. It was a tight fit but they just got in.

"Right," said Boox. "Let yourself go!"

"WWWUUURRRRRRRRAAAAAAAA-AGH!!!!!!!!" went the Worm, and the furnaces blazed away. The men came back to work, and all the people of Middlesbrough came out and danced in the streets, a sight never seen before or since. Boox had tamed the Lambton Worm!

Boox says that the Worm is still down there in the cellars, but as he's getting old they only use him for emergencies now. So if you go to Middlesbrough you might ask after him. But don't be surprised if they pretend to know nothing about it. They like to keep themselves to themselves around there.

DOCTOR BOOX

AND THE STRANDED WHALE

After his adventure with the Lambton Worm Boox decided that he owed himself a holiday. So he took the gorilla and the dogs to the coast.

"What I fancy," said Boox, "is a bit of fishing off South Shields Pier."

But when they got out of the train at South Shields, what did they see but a great crowd of people. It seemed as though all the people of South Shields were there.

"What's all the fuss about?" said Boox.

"Oh, Doctor Boox, Doctor Boox!" they said. "It's a stranded whale!"

"Back in the train, lads," said Boox.

"But you *must* help," said the people.

"I'm on *holiday*," said Boox. "Anyway, I'm not a whale man. I'm a Worm man."

"Please, Doctor Boox," they said.

"Oh, all right then," said Boox grumpily.

When he got down to the pier and saw the whale he nearly fell down in amazement. Whales are big things at the best of times and this one was a very big whale as whales go. It was nearly as long as South Shields pier. It looked at Boox sadly out of its small wet eyes.

"Never mind, whale," said Boox kindly. "Boox will see you all right."

Boox and the gorilla got up on the whale to take stock of things. They walked right down to the tail and back up to its head. It was so long that they were quite tired by the end of the walk and Boox sat down on its head to think. He thought for a long time. Then he said:

"We've got to make him slippery. That's the answer."

Then he stood up on the whale and all

the people crowded round.

"People of South Shields," said Boox importantly. "Get grease!"

All the people of South Shields went off to get grease.

The men came back with all the hair cream and car engine oil in South Shields, the children came back with all the cod liver oil and bicycle oil in South Shields, and their mothers came back with all the butter and dripping and washing-up liquid in South Shields.

"Slap it on," said Boox, and they covered the whale until it was shining and slippery from head to tail.

"Now push!" said Boox. They pushed. The whale moved about an inch and then stopped.

"Get out the custard creams," said Boox sadly. The gorilla took out all Boox's custard cream biscuits and smeared the cream on the whale.

"Push again," said Boox. Every man, woman and child in South Shields pushed. Boox pushed. The gorilla pushed. The dogs pushed. And the whale began to slide! Faster and faster it went. . . .

"Easy does it," said Boox, and with a great soft PLOP the whale was back in the sea, and a big wave ran softly up South Shields beach. All the people of South Shields cheered.

"Good old Boox!"

But the whale didn't swim away. It stayed close to the pier, looking at Boox in a meaning way. Boox thought.

"You know what?" he said. "I think he wants to give us a lift. Coming, lads?"

And Boox, the gorilla and the dogs stepped on to the whale's back while the people of South Shields stared in astonishment.

"Full speed for London," said Boox. "Anyone know how to steer a whale?"

In London, great crowds of people gathered on the Thames Embankment.

They were waiting to see the wonderful sight. Would Boox make it? Then the ships' sirens boomed in the distance, the cannons roared, and up the Thames came the great whale, cruising slowly and majestically under London Bridge, with the dogs barking, the gorilla beating his chest, and Boox waving his hat to the crowd.

"Good old Boox!" the shout went up. "The great whale doctor!"

Boox smiled his modest smile.

"It was nothing," said Boox.